Reggie
the Littlest Reindeer

CHEX BOOKS NEW YORK

Far, far away in a northern
land covered in ice and snow,
there lived a little reindeer
named Reggie.
Reggie was much smaller than the
other reindeer. This made him
feel very shy.
"I wish I wasn't so small,"
sighed Reggie. "Then I could play
with the other reindeer."

But Reggie had another wish,
something that he wanted more
than anything else in the world.
"I wish . . . I wish I could help
pull Santa's sleigh," said Reggie.
"Maybe you will, one day,"
said his mother.
"But soon it will be Christmas and
I'm so little," sighed Reggie.
"Then first you must wait until you
have grown up," replied his mother.

The other reindeer were much bigger than Reggie. They were very excited at the thought of helping Santa pull the sleigh.

"I wonder who will be chosen to help this year?" asked one. "I think it should be the strongest."

"No, it should be the fastest," said another.

"We will hold a contest," said a wise, old reindeer. "That's the best way to choose who should pull the sleigh."

Reggie had been listening to the other reindeer. This was his chance to help pull Santa's sleigh!
"May I enter the contest, too?" he asked, shyly.
"If you want to," said one reindeer. "But you'll never win. You're far too small!"

The first event was a race.
Reggie stood with the other
reindeer on the starting line.
"The first two reindeer to run
to that tree and back will be the
winners," said the judge.
"On your mark, get set, go!"
Reggie ran as fast as he could
but he couldn't keep up with
the others. His legs were far too
short and he watched sadly as
the other reindeer ran past him.

"Perhaps I'll be better at the
next contest," said Reggie.
He watched as a rope was tied
between two trees. One by one
the reindeer jumped over it.
When it was Reggie's turn
he took a long run and jumped.
Poor Reggie! His little legs
caught on the rope and he
landed on the ground with
a big bump!
"Tough luck, Reggie!" called
the judge. "You're just too little!"

"The test of strength is my last chance," said Reggie. "If only I can win."

"This is Santa's sleigh," said the judge. "All you have to do is pull it as far as you can." Little Reggie was tied to the sleigh. But no matter how hard he tried, he could not move it. He was so unhappy.

"Never mind," said Reggie's mother. "You can always try again next year."

The next day, the winners were announced. Reggie watched sadly as the six fittest and strongest reindeer walked proudly over to the sleigh.
It was filled to the top with presents of all shapes and sizes. "I wish I could go, too," sighed Reggie. "It must be so exciting to help Santa deliver all those presents."

Suddenly a great cheer went up.
"Here comes Santa!" cried Reggie.
"Greetings, my friends!"
cried Santa Claus as he strode
toward them. "It's good to see
you all again!"
He quickly checked the sleigh
then tied the reindeer to it.
"We really must be going,"
said Santa, smiling. "We have
a long night ahead of us!"

Reggie looked sadly at the sleigh before it set off. Then just as he was turning to go home, he saw the leading reindeer slip and fall into a snowdrift.

"Oh, no!" cried Santa.

"Now what are we going to do? There are so many presents to deliver and not enough reindeer to pull the sleigh!"

Then Santa saw a little reindeer standing in the distance.

"Reggie!" he cried. "You are just what we need! Will you help to pull my sleigh?"

Reggie could hardly believe his ears. His special Christmas wish was about to come true!

"Oh, yes!" he cried and the other reindeer smiled as Reggie was placed at the front of Santa's sleigh. They all knew how much Reggie wanted to help.

Reggie stood proudly at the front, his eyes shining brightly.

"At last," said Santa. "Now we can deliver all the presents."

He sprinkled the reindeer with magic dust and Reggie suddenly felt lighter.

"I can fly!" he cried.

Reggie's mother watched proudly as the sleigh climbed into the air with Reggie leading the way.

What a night Reggie had!
The reindeer stopped at every
house and Santa dropped down
the chimney with his sack
of presents. At last the
reindeer arrived home
as it was getting light.
"Thank you, all!" cried Santa.
"Now everyone can wake up
to a merry Christmas!"
Then Santa smiled and said,
"And a special thank you to
Reggie, the littlest reindeer!"
Reggie had never been so happy!

Say these words again

shy	deliver
Christmas	judge
smile	jump
proudly	dark
contest	night
front	true
race	wish